I
ALWAYS
Love

THAT MOMENT
WHEN...

SUDDENLY

You FEEL

a puff of breath . . .

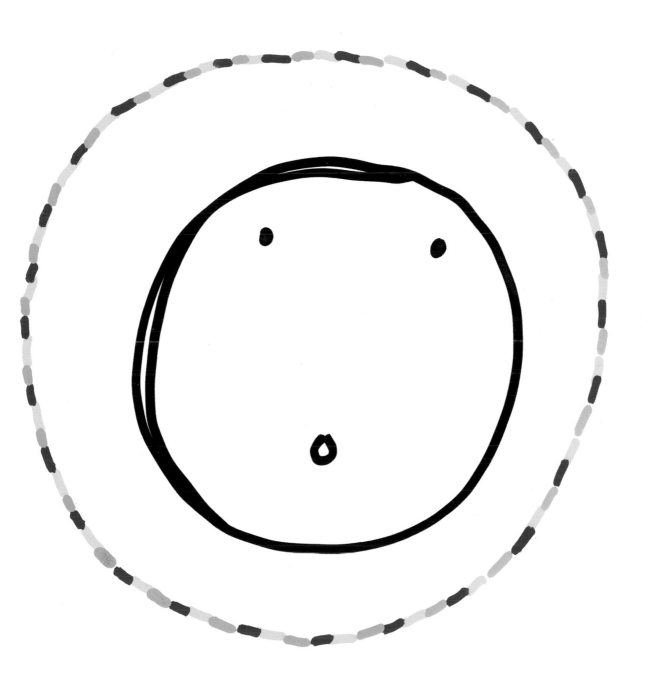

a
ficent
ling!

HMM . . .

BUT

JUST WHAT

is

AN

IDEA

?

AT FIRST,
YOU REALLY
AREN'T SURE

BUT You
START
LOOKING.

AND LOOKING . . .

and looking...

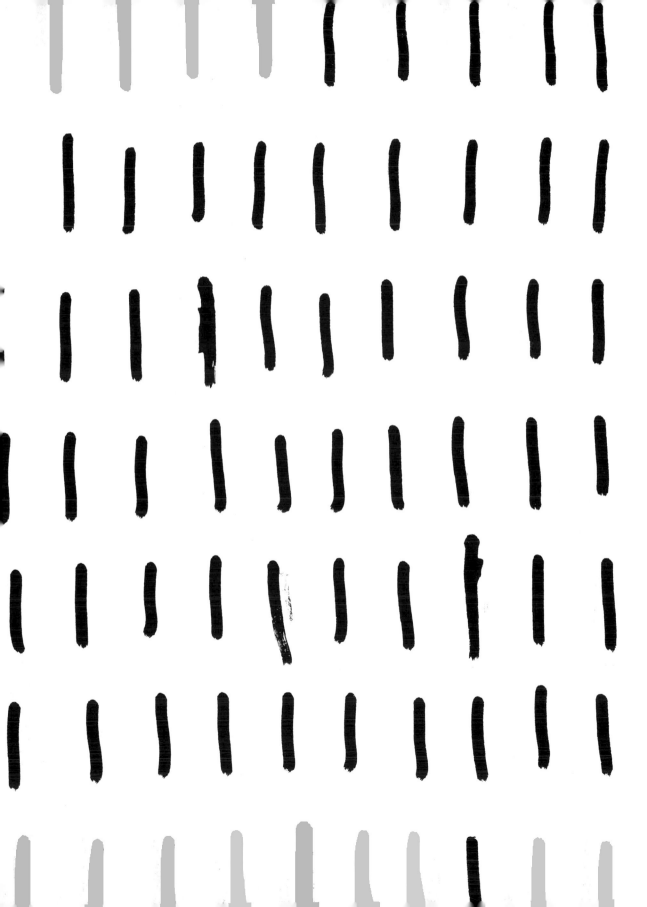

SO YOU KEEP ON LOOKING . . .

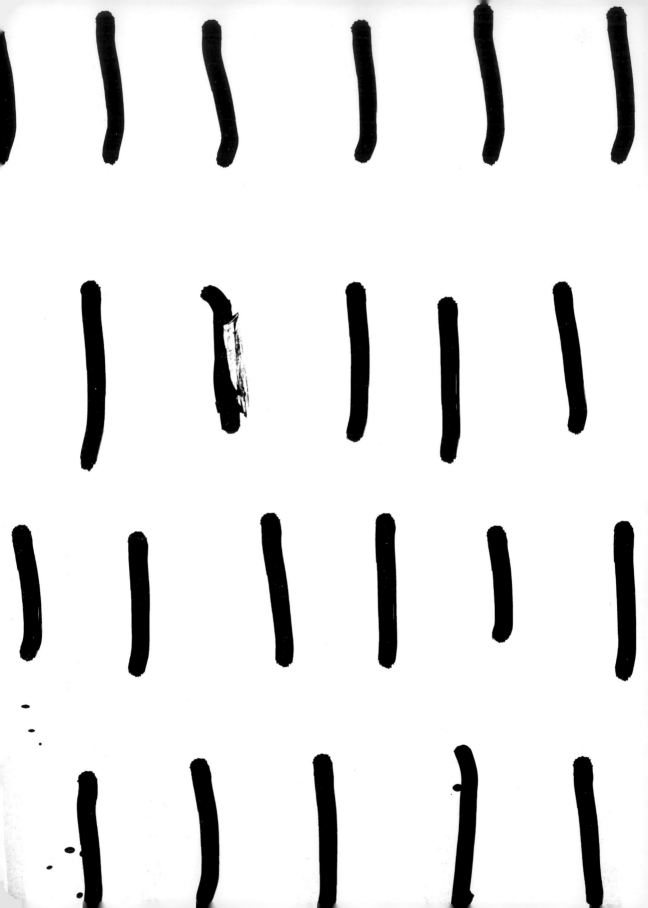

SOME MORE

(it can get a bit Boring)

AND THEN SUDDENLY . . .

OH!

It's
New.

It's
Different.

There's
Nothing
Like it.

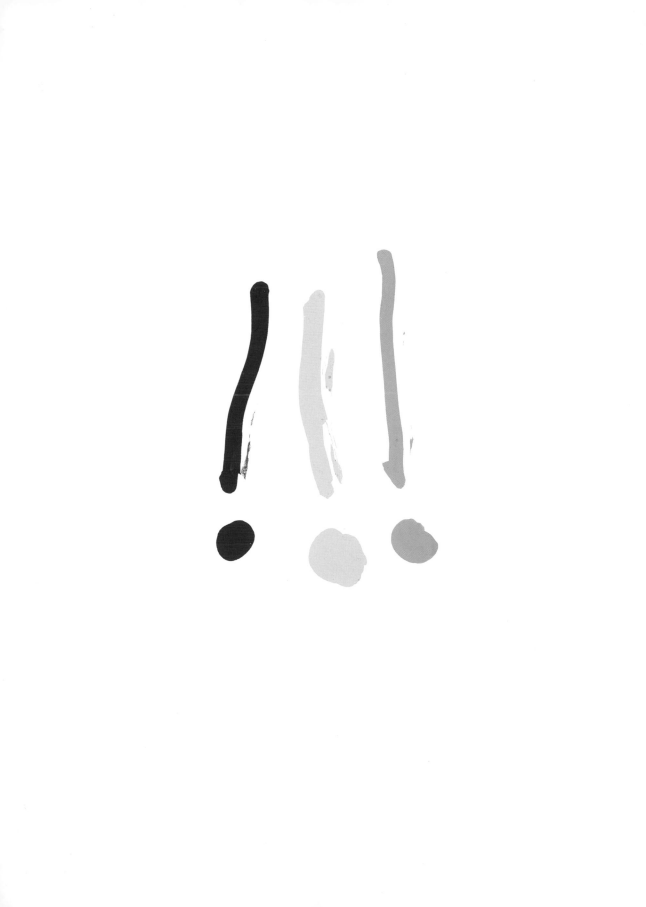

IT'S A
LITTLE LIKE
FINDING
A SEED,

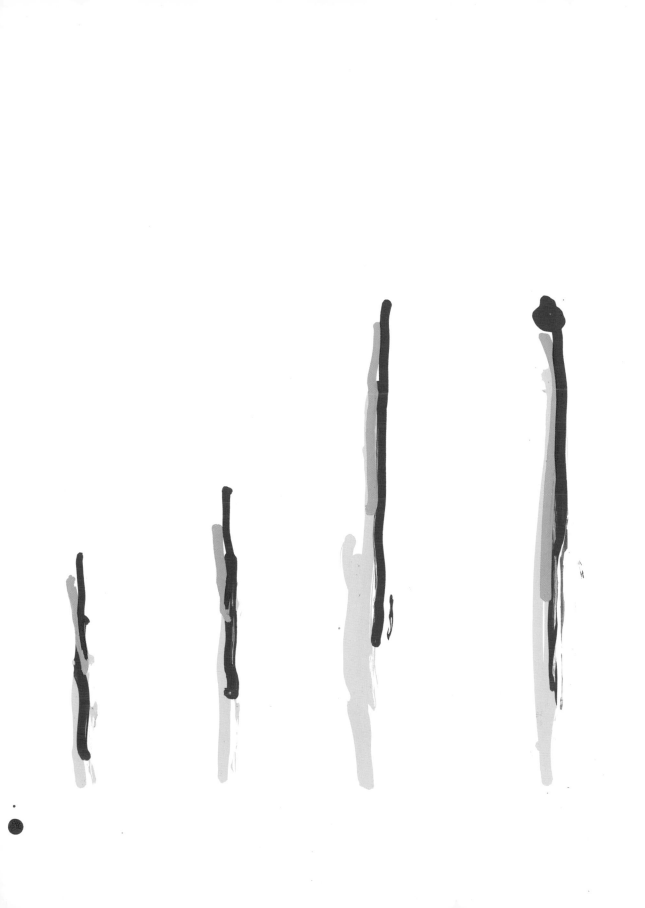

WHICH GROWS and
GROWS and GROWS...

AND WHAT DO

YOU DO

ONCE

YOU'VE FOUND

AN

IDEA?

OFTEN THE IDEAS

COME *Rushing,*

THEY CAN BE A BIT

Messy,

and

Bubbly...

iT'S TIME

TO GET TO

WORK!

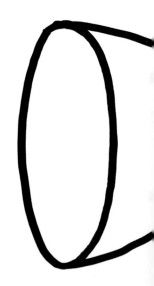

MAKE
START AGAIN,
EXPLORE.

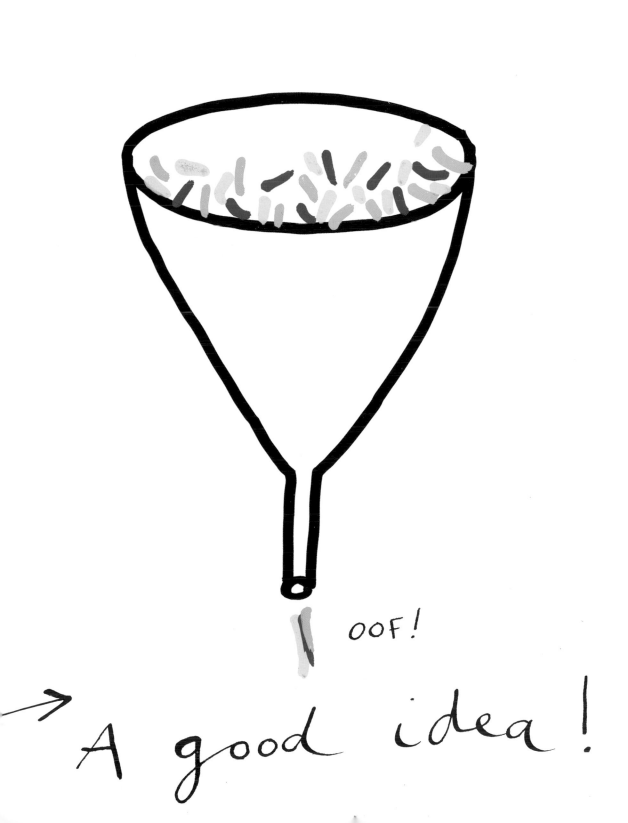

OOF!

→ A good idea!

AND
Right Away
YOU KNOW IT'S good
BECAUSE IN EVERY

good idea

THERE'S ALWAYS

A SEED OF

Madness.

So

HOW DO YOU

Find

and

Cultivate

THOSE

SEEDS ?

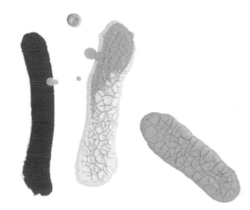

THEY´RE There,

EVERYWHERE

IN THE WORLD

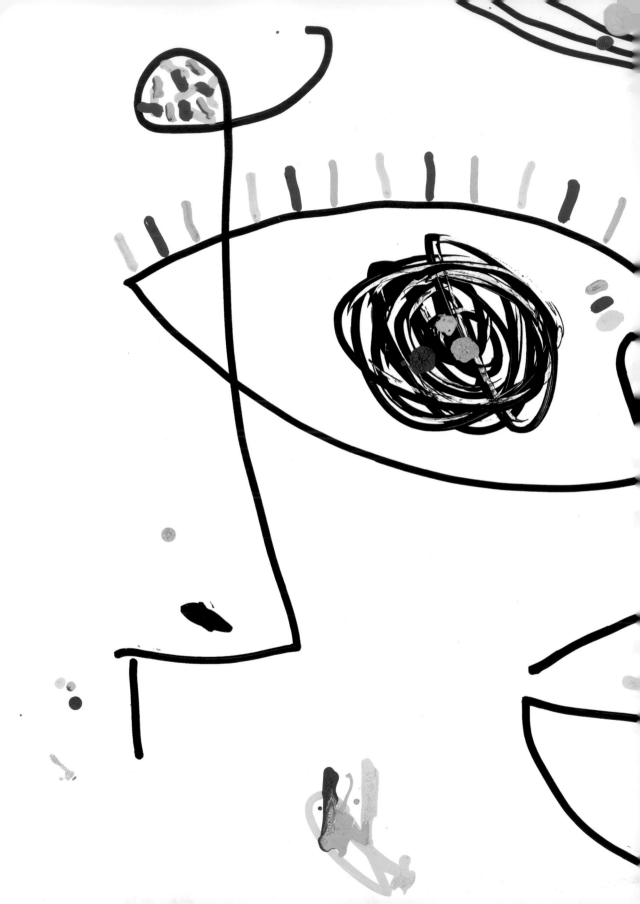

BE CURIOUS, LOOK, LISTEN, TOUCH, TASTE, SMELL, LEARN...

BECAUSE EVERYTHING
THAT YOU DISCOVER
WILL FIND
IT'S WAY
INTO YOUR BRAIN.

AND THEN
one day,
WHILE YOU'RE
STILL LOOKING...

SOME OF THE SEEDS

WILL CLUSTER TOGETHER

And

Then . . . .

BUT WHY

LOOK

FOR ALL

THOSE

iDEAS ?

MAYBE JUST FOR THE FUN OF IT ?

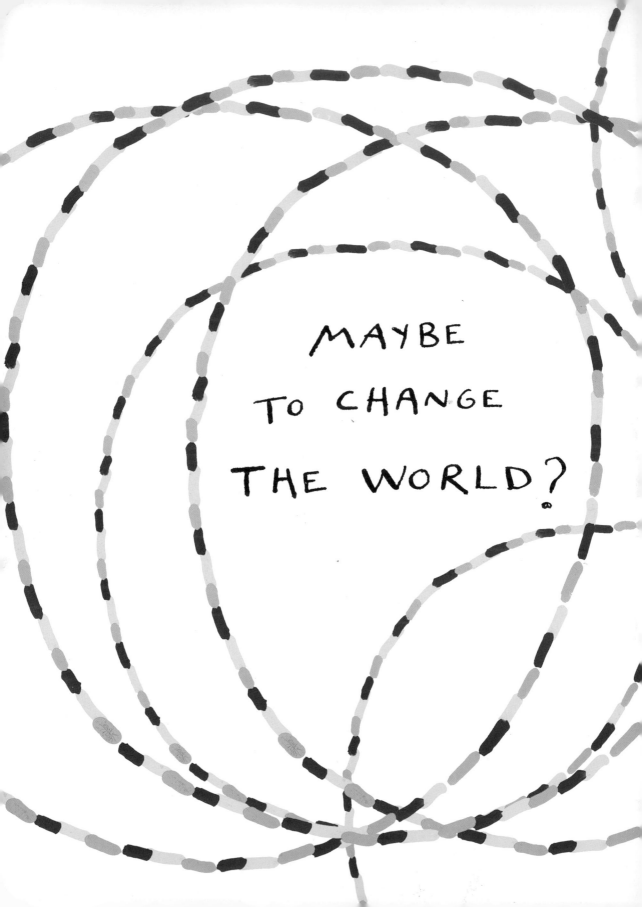

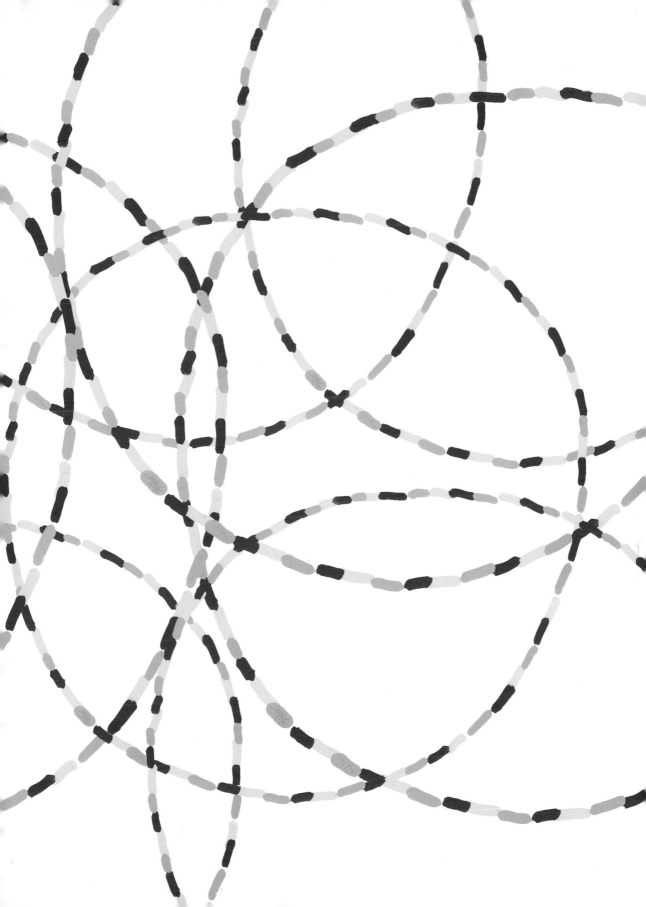

IN ANY CASE,
THERE'S ONE
THING
I'VE LEARNED:

WITH

LOOKING...

And
So
IF YOU LOOK,
YOU, TOO . . .
?

OTHER IDEAS BY THE AUTHOR WHICH HAVE APPEARED IN BOOK FORM:

PRESS HERE   MIX IT UP!   LET'S PLAY!

PRESIONA AQUÍ   ¡MÉZCLALO BIEN!   SAY ZOOP!

... AND A FEW OTHER IDEAS:

PRESS HERE THE GAME   PRESS HERE THE APP

ZAZAZOOM!

First published in the United States of America in 2019 by Chronicle Books LLC.
Originally published in France in 2018 by Bayard Éditions under the title "J'ai une idée."

Text and illustrations copyright © 2018 by Bayard Éditions.
English translation copyright © 2019 by Chronicle Books LLC.

Library of Congress Cataloging-in-Publication Data available.
ISBN 978-1-4521-7858-5

Manufactured in China.

FSC
www.fsc.org

MIX
Paper from responsible sources
FSC™ C104723

Translated by Christopher Franceschelli.
Original French edition design by Sandrine Granon.
Handprint/Chronicle Books design by Amelia Mack.
Hand lettered by the author and augmented by type set in Hervé Tullet Whimsy.
The illustrations in this book were rendered in paint.

10 9 8 7 6 5 4 3 2 1

Handprint Books
an imprint of Chronicle Books LLC
680 Second Street
San Francisco, California 94107

www.chroniclekids.com
www.herve-tullet.com